Robert and the Instant Millionaire Show

by Barbara Seuling
Illustrated by Paul Brewer

A
LITTLE APPLE
PAPERBACK

SCHOLASTIC INC.

New York Toronto London Auckland Sydney
Mexico City New Delhi Hong Kong Buenos Aires

To Caleb Mansfield, who shared his story
—B. S.

To Tony Jacobson, Laura Tillotson,
and John Grandits
—P. B.

ISBN 0-439-35376-9

12 11 10 9 8 7 6 5 4 3 2 1   2 3 4 5 6/0

Printed in the U.S.A.
First Scholastic printing, February 2002

Contents

A Million Dollars   1

Weird & Wacky Facts   6

Class Project   11

Galloping Gertie   17

Leonardo da Vinky   21

The $125,000 Question   26

The Phone Call   33

Over Eighteen   45

Oops!   49

A Million Dollars

"Listen to this," said Robert, reading from his notebook. "Some lizards are born with no eyes." He took a sip of orange juice as he waited for a response.

"Get out of here," said Charlie, slurping the last mouthful of cereal from his bowl. "Nothing is born with no eyes."

"Stop slurping," said their mother. "Eat slowly. It's better for your digestion."

"It's true," said Robert. "It's in *Weird & Wacky Facts #33*. Here's another one: Earthworms grow to eleven feet long in Australia."

Charlie sprang up from his seat and grabbed his book bag. "Gotta go. Hockey practice today. I'll be home late."

Before anyone could say anything, Charlie was out the door and gone. Robert read his mom one more fact before he got up.

"Mom, listen. People used to think a runny nose meant your brain was leaking."

His mom smiled and put her coffee cup down. "Very interesting, Robert, but save the book for later. Paul is waiting on his corner for you."

Robert put the book of facts in his book bag and hurried out the door. He and his best friend, Paul, were trying to see how smart they could get by memorizing all the facts their heads could hold. Then they could get on *The Instant Millionaire* show and make a million dollars.

A couple of weeks ago, he and Paul had mailed in a postcard to *The Instant Million-aire*, asking to be contestants. They used an old postcard Robert had found in the stationery drawer. It had a picture of Niagara Falls on the front.

"What would you do with a million dollars?" Paul had asked him then.

"I'd get a computer. I have to use my mom's now. I'd buy a gazillion packs of gummy bears and . . . an electric guitar."

"An electric guitar?" said Paul. "You don't play the guitar."

"Oh. Well, I can take lessons, if I have a million dollars," said Robert. "What about you? What would you get?"

"Me? Oh, lots of paints and brushes like a real artist. And maybe a mountain bike. I like that new electronic game, *Asteroid Attack,* but if I get it, Nick would probably destroy it." Nick was Paul's little brother, who got into Paul's things sometimes.

It was fun planning what they would do with a million dollars. They would share it because they were going to be each

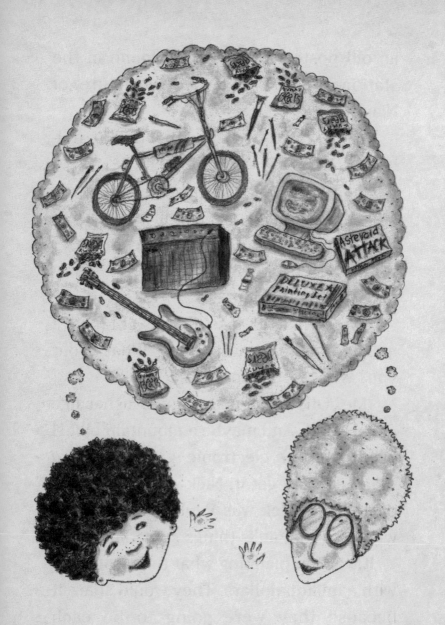

other's "Instant Buddy." You were allowed to have an Instant Buddy—someone to help you with your answers. They would be each other's Instant Buddy, because they were best friends, and because they were both going to memorize all the *Weird & Wacky Facts*.

Weird & Wacky Facts

" **G**ood morning, class," said Mrs. Bernthal as the children filed into the room. A new word was written in big letters on the chalkboard. Mrs. Bernthal gave them a new word to practice every day. They had to use the word three times during the day in conversation. Today's word was *ambitious*.

"I'm ambitious to become a famous artist," said Paul.

"I'm ambitious to read all the facts in the *Weird & Wacky Facts* series and memorize them," said Robert. Ever since he had met writer Frank Farraday during an author visit to his class, Robert wanted to know about everything. That's the kind of contestant they liked on *The Instant Millionaire*.

"I answered questions up to the $500 level last week," he told Paul at lunchtime.

Paul was impressed. "I only got up to $250," he said.

"We have to be ambitious and reach a higher level this week," said Robert.

Paul nodded. "Yeah."

The amount of money increased with each new level. The questions got harder and harder. Robert couldn't wait for next week's show. That was the hardest part of all. Waiting. The good part was that he had time to memorize a lot more facts. He was going to read and memorize all the books in the *Weird & Wacky Facts* series. He had almost all of them. The only ones missing were #11 and #23.

Lester Willis sat down at their lunch table.

"Hi, Lester," said Robert, taking out his *Weird & Wacky Facts #33.*

"Hi, guys," said Lester. "What are you doing?"

"Memorizing facts," said Robert, "so we can get really smart."

"Cool," said Lester. "I have one of those books."

"Bring it in and practice memorizing facts with us," said Robert. "It's fun."

"Okay," said Lester. He took his sandwich out of a brown paper bag and bit into it.

Later that afternoon, Mrs. Bernthal put a box on her desk. It was the familiar box that their book club books always came in. Robert and Paul had both ordered the latest *Weird & Wacky Facts* book, #34.

"You are going to be the smartest boys in the school," Mrs. Bernthal said with a smile.

Susanne Lee Rodgers got three books. Two were stories that had won some kind of medal. The third was a book about Amelia Earhart, a pilot. Susanne looked at the books in Robert's and Paul's hands.

"You should read some good books sometime," she said, looking at the boys as though they were bugs. Robert couldn't help grinding his teeth when Susanne Lee looked at him like that.

"This is a good book," said Paul. "It's excellent."

Susanne Lee just walked back to her table, her hair bouncing.

"What's her problem?" said Robert.

"Maybe she thinks we will become smarter than she is."

Robert thought of what Mrs. Bernthal had said. "Hey, Paul," he said. "Do you think that's possible?"

"What?" said Paul.

"That we could be as smart as—or smarter than—Susanne Lee?"

"I don't know," said Paul.

Robert wondered how Susanne Lee got so smart. She didn't even read *Weird & Wacky Facts*.

Class Project

"I'd like your attention, class," said Mrs. Bernthal when they settled in the next morning. There were pictures of famous bridges tacked up on the bulletin board. Robert recognized the Brooklyn Bridge. His family drove over that bridge when they visited Coney Island and the aquarium.

"What does a bridge do?" Mrs. Bernthal asked. That seemed pretty easy.

"It crosses a river," Lester Willis called out. Lester always called out. No matter how many times Mrs. Bernthal told him to raise his hand, he still shouted out whatever he had to say.

Mrs. Bernthal called on Susanne Lee, who always raised her hand. "A bridge lets you cross from one place to another," said Susanne Lee.

"Right," said Mrs. Bernthal.

Mrs. Bernthal talked about all kinds of bridges, even the bridge of your nose and the bridge on a violin. She said some people had artificial teeth called bridges, because they crossed from one tooth to another.

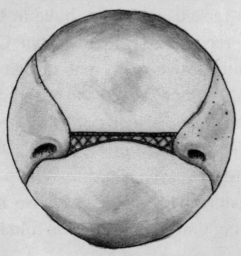

"We're going to learn about the kind of bridges that people build to walk or ride across," Mrs. Bernthal said. "I want you to choose a study partner for the next two weeks."

At their table, Robert and Paul did a high five. They knew they would be partners.

"You may study any bridge you like," said Mrs. Bernthal. "Do a report on it. Explain what kind of bridge it is and how it is made. Make a model of it and tell us why you chose that bridge."

"What bridge do you want to do?" Paul asked Robert.

"I don't know," said Robert. "Let's find one that's really unusual."

"Unusual how?" asked Paul.

"I don't know," Robert said, scratching his head. "I want ours to be different."

"Come over to my house after school tomorrow," said Paul. "We'll check out

13

bridges on the Internet." Paul always had good ideas. He also had his own computer.

"Did you know that the kiwi bird has no wings?" said Robert at dinner that night.

Mr. Dorfman's eyebrows went up as he chewed on a chicken wing, but he didn't say a word.

"That's a pretty useless bird, then," said Charlie. "It might as well be a cat."

"Have some broccoli, Robert," said Mrs. Dorfman.

Robert put a piece of broccoli on his plate. "In some places, people use feathers for money." He took a bite of his drumstick.

"I'd like to go to a place like that," said Robert's mom. "First I would collect all the duck feathers in Van Saun Park."

"How was practice today?" Robert's dad asked Charlie.

"Great," said Charlie, wolfing down a piece of corn bread. "I made two goals. Coach said he wants me to do some work with weights to strengthen my legs."

"What's wrong with your legs?" asked Mrs. Dorfman.

"Nothing," said Charlie. "It's just what hockey players do so they can skate faster and better. I think Coach might make me captain next year."

Robert's dad looked pleased. "That's terrific," he said. He turned to Robert. "And how's the Instant Millionaire?"

"Fine. I'm almost finished memorizing book #33."

Robert was glad his father had asked. Memorizing facts was hard work, after doing homework, and working on projects, and feeding Fuzzy, his pet tarantula, and his two doves, Flo and Billie. His head hurt sometimes from so much remembering.

Galloping Gertie

Robert and Paul had been working on their bridge report for an hour already. Paul sat at his computer, clicking away. Pages and pages on all kinds of bridges were taped to the walls. More papers were on the bed. There was the history of bridges. There were famous bridges. There were pictures of the oldest bridge, the longest bridge, the bridge that had the most traffic. And they still hadn't decided which bridge they would work on.

Robert got up to stretch. He wandered over to the bookshelf and picked up a dark blue cardboard folder. The folder opened like a book and showed each state and its new quarter plus state birds, mottoes, and flowers. New Jersey's state flower was the violet. The state bird was the goldfinch. The motto was "Liberty and Prosperity." Robert noticed that the cardinal appeared as the state bird for several states. He put the quarter collection back on the shelf.

"We can do London Bridge," said Robert, going back to the pages on Paul's bed. "The one that was in the old nursery rhyme. Remember? 'London Bridge is falling down, falling down, falling down. . . .'"

"We could, but it doesn't say anything about it really falling down. Now, *that* would be interesting," said Paul.

"It's time to relinquish your seat," said

Robert, using Mrs. Bernthal's latest word. "Let me try it."

Robert followed one link after another. "Look!" He found a pontoon bridge. "This bridge floats on the water," he said. Paul agreed that it had possibilities. Robert printed out that page.

He went back to surf some more. He found a bridge in Tacoma, Washington, that had twisted and turned so badly when the wind blew that it tore itself in two. There were pictures of it right on the computer screen. You could get seasick just from looking at them.

"Paul. Take a look. This is great."

Paul hooted when he saw it. "They called it Galloping Gertie!" he said.

"Let's do this one," said Robert.

Paul agreed. They had their bridge. It was not only a bridge. It was a bridge disaster! Cool.

Leonardo da Vinky

On Saturday, Paul came over on his bike to work on the model of Galloping Gertie. Robert's mom went off to the flea market, as she did every Saturday morning.

"I'll be back in time to fix you boys lunch," she called to them. "If you need a snack, there are some apple muffins in the fridge. And juice drinks."

"Okay, Mom," said Robert. He wished the muffins were homemade, like at Paul's house, but at least there was something to eat if they got hungry.

They spent the morning constructing a bridge that looked like the one in the pictures. Twice it collapsed, and they had to start all over again. They used all kinds of building materials. It was Paul's idea to use spaghetti boxes for the two towers that held the cables. Robert put the spaghetti into a plastic bag so they could use the boxes.

Paul found some rope they could use for the cables. With plenty of glue and tape, they held the pieces together. They connected old toy train tracks and used them for the roadway that carried cars across. By the time Robert's mom got home and made lunch, their version of Galloping Gertie was beginning to look pretty good.

They had melted cheese sandwiches for lunch. Robert's mom sat down with them and ate one, too.

"So how are you doing with your project?" she asked.

"Which one?" asked Paul.

"Oh. Didn't you say you had to build a bridge?"

"Yes," said Paul. "But I thought maybe you were asking about *The Instant Millionaire*. The bridge is okay so far."

"Well, how is the Instant Millionaire project going, then?"

"Great!" said Robert, before Paul could answer. "You want to hear some more facts?"

"Sure," said Mrs. Dorfman.

"You go first, Paul," said Robert.

Paul started. "Even if there are 80,000 bees in one hive, only one of them, the queen, can be a mother." He looked at Robert, signaling for him to go next.

"A famous artist named Leonardo da Vinky wrote all his notes backward so nobody could read them," Robert said.

Mrs. Dorfman smiled. "Very good," she said, "but it's da Vinci, Robert, with a *ch* sound, not a *k*."

"Oh. Thanks." Robert was pleased that his mom was listening to them. "Did you like those facts?"

"Yes, I liked them very much."

Robert walked Paul to the door.

"We've got to get up to $1,000 this week," said Paul.

"Let's memorize ten new facts by to-morrow," said Robert.

"Okay," said Paul. "Do you think memo-rizing facts really makes us smarter?"

"I don't know," said Robert, "but Mrs. Bernthal said so."

The $125,000 Question

Aunt Julie and Uncle Dan came for dinner on Sunday. At first, Robert thought he would be trapped for the day listening to dull grown-up talk. Or worse, sports talk, if Charlie had anything to do with it. But he was surprised.

"What's this?" asked Uncle Dan, reaching from the big overstuffed chair to the coffee table. He picked up one of Robert's *Weird & Wacky Facts* books.

"Oh, nothing," said Robert. "Just a book of facts."

"I used to love these when I was a kid," said Uncle Dan. "*Ripley's Believe It or Not* was in the Sunday papers, and there were whole books of Ripley's facts, too."

"Robert seems to be obsessed with odd facts," said Mr. Dorfman, winking at Robert.

Robert was not sure "obsessed" was a good thing to be, since he didn't know what the word meant, but it couldn't be too bad, since his dad winked.

"Well, I think a boy's got a right to have a passion for some things," said Uncle Dan. "I had baseball cards and comic books and G.I. Joe. They were all pretty important to me. And I didn't turn out so badly." He laughed. Robert's dad laughed, too.

"I guess that's true enough," he said.

After dinner, the women started telling family stories. Robert loved this part of their visits, especially when his mom and Aunt Julie talked about when they were kids. They mentioned things Robert had never heard of—pet rocks, mood rings, and tie-dyeing (whatever that was).

Before they knew it, it was seven-thirty.

"Look at the time, Dan," said Aunt Julie. "We have an hour's drive to Connecticut. We'd better get going."

"Why don't you stay and watch *The Instant Millionaire* with us?" asked Robert's mom. "Robert insists we see it. You won't get home in time to watch it yourselves. I'll put on another pot of coffee."

They agreed and settled into the living room. The smell of brewing coffee soon filled the house. Robert loved that smell. He had tasted coffee once, but it didn't taste as good as it smelled.

The music played, and the lights flashed blue and green and purple. In a little spot in the center of the screen was Todd Edwards, the host.

"Welcome to another show, ladies and gentlemen, where ordinary people like YOU"—he pointed right at the camera—"can become instant millionaires!"

Tonight a woman got up to the $50,000 level. The suspense built as she answered the question: What do you call the implement that you use to turn over hamburgers? Is it a ladle, a tureen, a spatula, or a whisk?

"A spatula?"

The woman got it right. Robert made a

mental note to add the word *spatula* to his word list. He liked the way it sounded.

By the time the coffee was ready, the woman had won $75,000, then $100,000. She was ready for the $125,000 question. Robert's parents and his aunt and uncle were just as excited as he was now. You could feel the tension when Todd Edwards asked, "Which bird is represented more than any other as a state bird?"

Robert gulped. He knew the answer. He had seen it in Paul's quarter collection. "The cardinal," he said. The clock ticked. The woman was sweating. She didn't know the answer. She had used up her three Instant Buddy turns. The buzzer went off.

"Oh, I'm sorry," said Todd Edwards. "It's the cardinal."

Everyone turned to Robert.

"Robert! How did you know that?" said Aunt Julie.

Robert shrugged and smiled politely. His mom and dad looked at him as if they weren't sure who he was.

"Yo, bro," said Charlie. "Not bad."

Wow. Even Charlie was impressed.

Aunt Julie and Uncle Dan left after the program was over. Robert went upstairs to call Paul. Wait until he told him he'd answered the $125,000 question!

The Phone Call

Getting the bridge to school was the hardest part. The model was glued to a large piece of cardboard. Robert carried it down the stairs from his room, slowly and carefully. He set it on the floor by the door while he slurped down a glass of juice and gobbled a toaster tart.

"Take your time, Rob," said his mom. Robert wiped the crumbs off his mouth and wiggled into his backpack straps. As he picked up the bridge model, his mom got up to open the door. "Just walk slowly," she said. "And good luck."

"Thanks," said Robert, balancing the board in front of him.

The bridge swayed as badly as the original Galloping Gertie had done. By the time Robert got to Paul's corner, his arms hurt from trying to keep the board straight.

"We both have to carry it," he said. "I don't think I can make it to school without having all our work collapse." Paul agreed and held up one side of the board. Since he was quite a bit taller than Robert, the board was on a slant.

"Why don't we use Nick's wagon?" asked Paul.

"Good idea," said Robert. They were close enough to Paul's house to get the wagon and still be in time for school.

Paul's mom came to the door. "What happened? Why aren't you in school?"

"Hi, Mrs. Felcher," said Robert. "We're having trouble carrying our bridge."

"Can we borrow Nick's wagon?" asked Paul.

"Sure, I guess so," said Paul's mom.

They laid the board down on the front step while Paul went into the garage to get the wagon. Meanwhile, Nick toddled up to his mom to see what was going on. Paul came out with the wagon. In it was a small portable fan.

"I thought we could use this," said Paul.

Robert put the model next to the fan. Nick ran over and tried to climb into the wagon.

"No, no, Nick," said Paul. "You can't go this time."

Nick howled. Mrs. Felcher picked him up, but he only screamed louder.

"Hey, Nick," said Robert, trying to calm him down, "we'll bring it back."

"Let's just go. Fast." Paul raced down the driveway with the wagon bouncing along behind him.

"Slow down," said Robert, about a block from Paul's house. "We don't want a bridge disaster until later."

Matt Blakey and Joey Rizzo did their report first, on the George Washington Bridge in New York City. Matt passed out photographs of the bridge that he had taken himself. The construction was made out of coat hangers, cardboard, and string. Joey rolled a tiny car over the bridge. Other toy cars and trucks were glued to the roadway.

Emily Asher and Kristi Mills showed something that looked like a house. Kristi talked about covered bridges while Emily walked around the room with their model.

"The roof kept the bridge clear of snow and ice," Kristi said. "That made it easier for horses to get across."

When it was their turn, Robert and Paul wheeled their bridge to the front of the classroom. They lifted it out of the wagon onto a table. Paul talked about suspension bridges and how they were built. Robert explained what had happened after the Tacoma bridge was completed.

"The wind made the bridge sway," he said. Paul turned on the fan to LOW. The rope cables on their bridge moved a little.

"The wind got stronger," said Robert, "and the bridge began to sway to and fro." Paul turned up the fan to MEDIUM. Nothing happened.

"It's a good thing cars stopped going across . . ." said Robert, giving Paul a sign. Paul turned the fan up to HIGH. ". . . because

there was a windstorm. Before long the bridge twisted itself in two and collapsed." The model blew over on its side.

Robert looked down at the bridge. "It really didn't fall over like this one did," he added. "It twisted like a crazy roller coaster. That's when they nicknamed the bridge 'Galloping Gertie.' It finally collapsed, and that was the end of it."

The class applauded. Robert and Paul took bows.

The rest of the morning went quickly as they watched and listened to the other bridge reports.

Robert was really hungry at lunchtime. He was about to take a bite of his sandwich when Lester bounced up.

"Hey, Rob," he said, plunking down across from Robert. "What's in your sandwich?"

"Baloney and cheese."

"What's in yours?" Lester asked Paul.

"Tuna fish."

"I got sardines," said Lester. Robert hated sardines. He even hated the smell of them. Lester opened his sandwich, and Robert tried not to make a face.

Lester took out a *Weird & Wacky Facts* book. The cover was ripped and the pages were worn, but Robert saw that it was #11—one of the two that he didn't have in his collection.

"Lester, where did you get that?" asked Robert.

"This? I don't know," said Lester. "It's been around the house for a long time."

"Don't you remember?"

Lester shrugged. "No. You want it?"

Robert gasped. "Really? You'd give me your book?"

"Sure. Maybe in return for your sandwich." Lester stared at Robert's baloney and cheese.

Robert looked down at his sandwich. He pushed it toward Lester.

"For a whole week," added Lester.

"It's a deal," Robert said.

Lester handed the book to Robert. "You can have this, too," said Lester, pushing his sardine sandwich across the table.

"Thanks," said Robert, not wanting to hurt Lester's feelings.

The minute the bell rang and Lester looked the other way, Robert tossed the sandwich in the trash.

When they got to Robert's house after school, Robert was starving. He grabbed a bag of chips and had just ripped them open when his mom walked in.

"Hi, boys," she said. "You got a phone call, Rob. From *The Instant Millionaire*."

Robert almost choked on a chip. "Mmrrot . . . mmffft . . . What . . . did they want?" He coughed to clear the chip from his throat.

"Well, when they asked for you, I said you were in school. When they found out how old you are, they said you could not be a contestant on the show. Contestants have to be over eighteen years old."

Robert's dream of fame and fortune came crashing down. Paul was pretty bummed out, too. They went up to Robert's room.

"Maybe we were too ambitious," said Robert, flopping down on the beanbag chair.

"Maybe we're not prominent enough," said Paul, using their new vocabulary word. He flopped down on the beanbag chair next to Robert. It was where they did their best thinking.

"Over eighteen!" said Robert.

Paul tossed up a chip and caught it in his mouth. "I didn't know you had to be old to get on the show," he said.

"By the time we're eighteen," said Robert, "there will probably be a gazillion more *Weird & Wacky Facts* books!"

Paul said, in a voice like a TV reporter, "Robert Dorfman and Paul Felcher, once members of Mrs. Bernthal's class, memorized every fact in the *Weird & Wacky Facts* series, except for books #23, #492, and #2,359."

Robert continued, "They were so ambitious that they went on to memorize the entire Encyclopaedia Britannica . . ."

"And the dictionary . . ." said Paul.

"And the *Guinness Book of World Records,* too . . ." Robert added.

"Before they relinquished their place in Mrs. Bernthal's class to become prominent world leaders," finished Paul.

Paul tossed another chip up in the air. They both went for it at the same time, mouths open. *BONK!*

"Ow!"

"Ouch!"

They rubbed their heads and looked at each other. Then they laughed so hard they rolled off the beanbag in a heap.

Over Eighteen

After Paul left, Robert thought again about *The Instant Millionaire*. Maybe they could find someone who was over eighteen who could go on the show for them. He or Paul could be that person's Instant Buddy, to help with the harder questions. But who would it be?

It had to be someone who knew a lot about everything. His dad knew a lot about math. Frank Farraday knew all there was to know about animals. But that wasn't enough. Robert needed someone who knew a lot about a gazillion different things.

At last he thought of the perfect person. Mrs. Bernthal! She knew everything. Robert thought about all the things Mrs. Bernthal knew. She knew lots of vocabulary words. She knew about Native Americans, Pilgrims, and presidents. She knew math and all the state capitals, and how to spell every word in the spelling book. She knew about rain forests, dinosaurs, plants, the flag, pollution, and more. She even knew about snakes. Mrs. Bernthal had bought them a beautiful green ribbon snake named Sally and taught them how to take care of her. And Mrs. Bernthal was over eighteen for sure.

Robert was so excited, he didn't even remember to call Paul first. He thumped downstairs to the den and opened the stationery drawer. He picked out another postcard from the bunch in the rubber band. This one was from the Luray Caverns in Virginia.

Next, he pulled out the telephone book and looked up Mrs. Bernthal's address and telephone number. He wrote on the left side of the postcard:

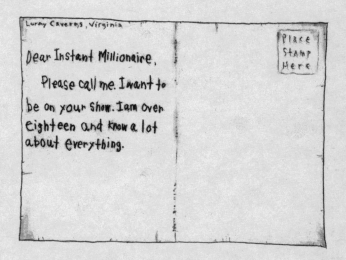

Underneath, he wrote Mrs. Bernthal's name, address, and telephone number. On the right side of the postcard, he wrote in the address of *The Instant Millionaire* show,

47

just as he had before. He found a stamp in the drawer and stuck it on the corner of the postcard.

He went back upstairs and put the postcard in his book bag to mail on the way to school in the morning.

Oops!

Robert was starving. Again he had had to give up his lunch for a sardine sandwich. Didn't Lester ever bring anything else for lunch? He grabbed a slice of American cheese and a juice drink from the refrigerator and went upstairs to check on his animals.

The birds twittered as Robert entered his room. "Hi, Flo. Hi, Billie." It was nice to have the doves greet him, especially when no one else was home. He opened the cage door and let them fly around the room for their exercise.

The phone rang. Robert went to answer it on the upstairs landing.

"Dorfman residence, Robert speaking." Robert answered the phone just as he had been taught to do.

"This is Mike Cosmo of Cosmo's Collectibles," said a man's voice. "Is Mrs. Dorfman there?" Robert told him she was not and asked if he could take a message.

"Tell her I'm the guy she met at the flea market Saturday. I want to buy her postcard collection. She'll know what I'm talking about." Mr. Cosmo spelled his name for Robert. "Tell her I will be at the flea market this coming Saturday if she's interested."

Uh-oh. Those postcards he used—could they have been from his mom's collection? He thought they were just old, leftover cards.

After he hung up, Robert went to the den and found the postcards in the stationery drawer again. He took off the rubber band and spread them out like a fan. The Grand Canyon. Miami Beach. Alaska. Mount Desert Island, Maine. The Badlands. Cheyenne, Wyoming. Salt Lake City, Utah. They were from all over the country.

He noticed this time that some of the cards had been written on, but they were to and from people Robert had never heard of.

When his mom came home, Robert gave her the message from Mr. Cosmo.

"That's great," she said. "I had a feeling those postcards were worth something."

With a funny feeling in his stomach, Robert asked, "What postcards was Mr. Cosmo talking about, Mom?"

"I've been saving old postcards for years," she told him. "I have quite a collection."

"The ones in the stationery drawer?"

"Yes. Plus a few shoe boxes full upstairs. I used to think I would travel to all the places on those postcards."

Robert gulped. It was getting harder to speak. "Did you?"

"No. I met your father, and he doesn't like to travel that much." Mrs. Dorfman sighed.

Robert tried to tell his mom about the two postcards he had used for *The Instant Millionaire,* but his voice wouldn't come out. What if they were worth a lot of money? Robert felt his stomach do a flip.

"I think we should have Chinese food tonight," said Robert's dad as he entered the room. "I'll go and pick it up. What does everyone want? The usual?"

"That's fine with me," said Robert's mom. "And you, Rob?" Robert shrugged. He wasn't very hungry, even for Chinese food.

"What's wrong, Rob?" asked his mom later, when the food came. He was poking the fried dumpling on his plate with his fork.

"Nothing," said Robert. He picked up the dumpling and nibbled around its edges. He put it back down.

"Are you sure?" said his mom. "You usually love fried dumplings."

"May I be excused?" Robert said.

His mom looked surprised. "Of course," she said. "Are you feeling all right?"

"Yes. I mean, no. I mean, yes. I'm just tired."

"Well, go on," said his mom. "If you get hungry later, we can heat up some leftovers for you."

Robert left the table and went up to his room. He lay on his bed and stared at the ceiling. How was he going to tell his mom what he had done? Maybe now Mr. Cosmo wouldn't want her postcard collection. Maybe his mom had lost out on a gazillion dollars because of what he'd done.

Robert rolled over on his stomach and wondered how many flea markets he'd have to walk through before he could replace his mom's postcards.

There was a knock on his door.

"Rob, I'm worried about you," said his mom, coming in. "Are you okay?"

Robert rolled over on his back again and sat up. "Mom, I used two of those postcards," he said.

"The postcards?" she repeated. "In the
desk?"

Robert nodded.

"How come?" She didn't seem angry.

"I thought they were just old, leftover cards," said Robert. "I needed to write postcards to someone."

"Ah," said his mom. "Of course. They were right there in the stationery drawer." She smiled. "They wouldn't have been sent to *The Instant Millionaire* now, would they?"

"Yes," Robert said. "Were they worth a lot of money?"

"Well, not a *lot* of money. I don't think two cards will make much of a difference to Mr. Cosmo, if that's what's worrying you."

"Oh, that's good," said Robert. He felt better. "How come you saved all those cards for so long and now you want to sell them?"

"I don't need them anymore," she said.

"How come?"

"I decided to stop dreaming and start doing," his mom answered.

56

"Doing? You mean go someplace?" Robert felt a stab of loneliness just at the thought of his mom leaving. He had missed her terribly the last time she had to go on a trip for her job.

"Not me alone. All of us. Maybe we'll go skiing this winter."

Robert actually thought that could be fun. Skiing was not like hockey, or baseball, or other jock sports. Skiing couldn't be much different from playing in the snow with his sled.

"All I have to do is convince your dad," said his mother.

"Oh, yeah. That won't be easy, will it?" said Robert. He thought of how his dad hated trips and loved his recliner and his videotape collection, neatly arranged in alphabetical order on a shelf in the den.

"Oh, I don't know," said his mom. She had a twinkle in her eye. "I found out there's going to be a convention of math and science teachers in Aspen, Colorado, this winter. If we can lure your dad to that, we can ski all day while he goes to stuffy old meetings. He can join us on the slopes if he gets bored with math."

Maybe Robert had to stop dreaming and start doing, too. *The Instant Millionaire* was dreaming. He didn't need a million dollars. He and Paul had plenty of fun without an electric guitar and a mountain bike. He ran to the telephone to call Paul and tell him.

BARBARA SEULING is a well-known author of fiction and nonfiction books for children, including several books about Robert. She divides her time between New York City and Vermont.

PAUL BREWER likes to draw gross, silly situations, which is why he enjoys working on books about Robert so much. He lives in San Diego, California, with his wife and two daughters.